ROSIE
AND
ROLLAND
in the *LEGENDARY* *SHOW-and-TELL*

by *JON BERG*

Owlkids Books

J.R. Clarke Public Library
102 E. Spring St.
Covington, Ohio 45318

D1482225

15.00

B3T

9/17

Rosie thought it would take forever for Ms. Fairfax to pick her.

Tomorrow was Friday. And every Friday was show-and-tell.

Maybe this would be the day.

"You'll get your chance sometime soon," her grandpa had said as he helped her pack her schoolbag that morning.

And so Rosie sat up straight and tall, hoping that her teacher would notice her.

Other kids waved their hands or said, "Me, me! Pick me!" Freddy Jones jumped up, like he did every week. But Ms. Fairfax had always told them to settle down and sit nicely, so that's what Rosie did...though she could feel her stomach bubbling inside her like Grandpa's kettle.

Finally, Ms. Fairfax spoke. "All right, Janice. Can you bring in something special to show the class?"

Freddy piped up quickly, "But, Ms. Fairfax, she's already brought something!"

"Oh, that's right," Ms. Fairfax said. "Okay, Freddy, you can bring in something tomorrow..." She looked around the room. "Rosie! Can you also bring something?"

Rosie finally breathed out. "Thank you!"

Rosie couldn't have been more excited to hear the bell for the end of the day. She packed up her things and headed for the door.

But before she could see it coming, she had walked into someone and fallen flat on her back.

It was Freddy Jones.

"Watch where you're going, Rosie Posie!" he said, staring down at her.

"Sorry, Freddy," she said. "And that's not my name," she finished as he walked away.

Rosie burst through her front door. Her best friend came bounding up to meet her. She knelt close to his face.

"Rolland! I got picked! I have to find something special to show at school tomorrow!"

He wagged his tail and yipped.

"But what to bring?"

They searched high and low, in and out, around and behind, up and down...nothing. At least, nothing that Rosie thought was special enough for show-and-tell.

Rolland brought Rosie an old wide-brimmed hat and placed it at her feet.

"Oh yes, that's Grandpa's. But I don't want to show a dusty old hat—they'll all laugh," she said. "Rolland, what will I do?"

Rosie picked up Rolland's ball and threw it for him. It bounced across the floor and got caught in the straps of her schoolbag.

"Oh, right—my homework."

She unzipped her bag and turned it upside down. Out dropped her lunch pail, library books, pencil case, and an old, tattered piece of paper: a map.

"Rolland, look..."

She turned it over, examining the writing and pictures. The map's edges were worn and ragged.

"Wow, this is special enough, right, boy? Where could this have come from? Where does it lead?"

She carefully spread the map out on the floor.
"I think I've seen this symbol before," she said
after a while, pointing to a circular design at the
bottom of the page. "In...Grandpa's study?"
She and Rolland raced up the stairs.
"Look around, boy," Rosie said.
"There!" She pointed at an especially high
cupboard. Stepping on a pile of books on the floor,
she scaled the shelves toward the mysterious
cabinet. Opening its doors, she peered inside.

"There's a...cave in here!"

Rolland darted back into the study. He came back
carrying Grandpa's hat.

"Really?" she said, putting on the hat. "All right." She took
a flashlight from her grandpa's drawer. "Let's go!"

The darkness was thick. Rosie turned on the flashlight.
"Rolland, there are drawings on the walls," she whispered.
They walked until they came to a fork in the cave. Rolland
sniffed each tunnel while Rosie turned to the map. She could see
that the path to the left would take them out. So on they walked.
Soon enough, she could see a spot of sky ahead. Rolland gave
a quick bark and bounded forward.

They emerged from the cave onto the edge of a mountainside. They both took a deep breath of fresh air. Before them was a valley full of lush jungle. Rosie pulled the map from her pocket.

She followed the path with her finger until it met a river. Rolland put his paw on the path. "Yes, boy, it looks like that's where we need to go. Let's find that river!"

Rolland led the way into the jungle. Insects flew around his head. Birds whirled and squawked above. His ears twitched with each new noise. Then...*SNAP!*

"What was that?" Rosie looked around.

But Rolland had already bounded ahead after the sound. Rosie ran after him...until suddenly her feet couldn't find ground. She fell head over heels down a hidden slope, tumbling into Rolland ahead of her. Tangled up, they rolled and rolled until they landed in a heap.

Then they heard it. Rolland's ears turned. Rosie sat up.

"That's the sound of water!"

They pushed through a thick maze of plants to find the river. Rosie squatted on a rock and pulled out the map again.

"We are somewhere along this river, and if we want to follow the path, we'll have to go with the current." She looked at Rolland. "It's too bad we don't have a boat." She sat down on the ground. "My feet can't take any more walking."

"*Rrruff!*"

"And all these bugs…"

"*RRRUFF!*" Rolland hopped down the other side of a boulder.

Rosie picked herself up and followed him. There she saw an old log. Rolland had dragged over a stick with a flat end.

"Of course! That will work!" said Rosie. "Good boy!"

She wrapped her arms around her dog's neck. They hopped on the log and took off, down the rolling jungle river.

The river started out running fast, but farther down the current slowed. Trees hung heavily over their heads.

"Rolland, did that rock just move?" The pair eyed the murky water. "That one over there did, too! And that one!"

Sure enough, it seemed like dark rocks were rising all around them. They were trapped.

"They're alligators!" Rosie cried.

One of the alligators snapped at Rolland, but he sprung off the log—and onto another gator. Bounding quickly, Rolland hopped from one gator to the next. They snapped at him but kept missing, biting each other's tails instead.

"Go, Rolland!" yelled Rosie, as she bopped a gator on the head with her paddle.

Jump! Leap! Bound! Rolland hopped back on
their log just in time to escape one last gator chomp.
Discouraged, the dazed and sore alligators finally
swam away.

"That was close. But our poor paddle..." said Rosie,
holding up the chewed and broken stick.

They had no choice but to drift down the river.

Their log eventually met a sandy bank. From there, the river broke into smaller streams. Weary and wet, Rosie and Rolland sat down on the shore.

"The river ends here, but so does the map," Rosie said, after a moment. "I'm going to see what's around."

She pushed herself up off the sand and looked through the trees at the edge of the jungle.

"Rolland! It's a pyramid. Let's see what's inside!"

"Hello? Is anybody home?" Rosie called out. There was no reply, just a faint echo.

A short tunnel led her and Rolland to a door that they pushed open together. They walked into a large, round room. It was cool and quiet. Entrances to five tunnels stood around them.

Rosie swung the flashlight. She watched as bugs crawled away from its beam.

"I don't know which way to go." She shone the light on a wall. "Wait! It looks like there's something behind here."

As they cleared away some vines from the wall, they discovered hidden pictures.

"It's some kind of story," she said. "They're walking in with torches, but then the torches go out..."

Rosie thought for a moment.

"I think we need to close that door."

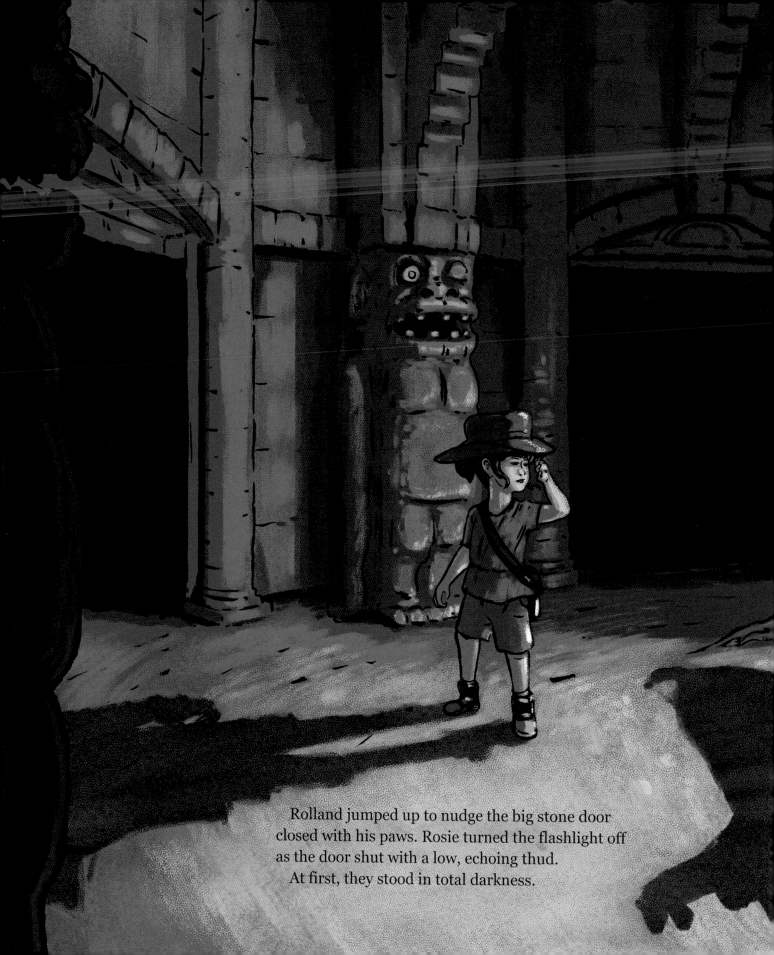

Rolland jumped up to nudge the big stone door
closed with his paws. Rosie turned the flashlight off
as the door shut with a low, echoing thud.
At first, they stood in total darkness.

"Hmm. Guess not, boy."

Rosie moved to turn the light back on...when it slowly started to happen.

"Oooooooo..."

One of the passageways began to glow gold, lit by hundreds of tiny rocks!

Rolland bounded over to the illuminated tunnel, with Rosie right behind.

With only the golden stones to guide them, they headed deeper into the pyramid. They followed the glow to a room where the ceiling got higher, and it looked as if they were back in the jungle. Vines and plants were everywhere.

Below them, down a shallow well, they could see a light even brighter than the one from the stones.

They both looked around for a way down. Rosie grabbed a nearby vine, tied it off to a rock, and lowered it into the hole. She tied another vine around her waist and then to Rolland.

"I'll be right behind you, boy."

Slowly they dropped down into the well.

At the end of the vine, they let go, landing in a room of blinding light. At the far end, two stone figures held up a throne. Sitting upon it was a great monkey. He looked like a king.

The monkey's expression was very calm, as if he had been sitting there for a long time. In his hands was what lit the entire room: a perfectly round, golden sun.

"Wow, Rolland. Look at that! This must be what the map was leading us to," Rosie said quietly. "It'll be the best show-and-tell ever."

J.R. Clarke Public Library
102 E. Spring St.
Covington, Ohio 45318

"*ARRROOOOOO!!*" Rolland interrupted, jumping in front of the monkey.

The monkey scowled and started to howl again:

"*YEEEEEOOOOO—*"
"*ARRRRROOOOOO!!*"

Rolland scampered behind the big king, startling him with another howl of his own. The monkey turned to try and face him, but Rolland was too quick.

"*ARRROOOOOO!!*"
"*ARRRRROOOOOOO!!*"

This time, the monkey dropped the ball from his hands. Now frightened, he scampered up a vine and out a hole in the roof.

"*Ruff!*" Rolland said, quite pleased with himself.

"You out-howled a howler!" said Rosie. She scooped up the ball and put it safely in her bag.

Rosie couldn't help feeling pleased by the new weight at her side. She placed a hand over her bag. "Time to get out of here," she said. "But where is the vine?"

"Hello, Rosie Posie. Looking for something?"

Rosie and Rolland looked up.

"Freddy? How...?"

Rolland started to growl. Freddy was holding the vine just out of their reach.

"You'll tie the treasure to this vine. I'll pull it up and then lower your vine back to you."

Rosie scowled. "This is *our* treasure. We solved the clues and found it."

"Fair enough." Freddy turned to leave. "That monkey might be back with some of his friends...but good luck!"

"WAIT!"

Rolland looked up at Rosie. He nudged her bag.

"Okay," she said. She tied the bag to the vine, and Freddy pulled it up.

"Thanks!" he said. "Here's your vine back!"

The vine fell limply in front of them in a pile.

"Hey! We had an agreement!" Rosie yelled.

"Deal shmeal, Rosie Posie! Oh, but here. You dropped something at school!"

He flew a paper airplane over to them, hitting Rolland in the nose.

"See you at show-and-tell!" Freddy hollered back from the passageway.

Rosie picked up the airplane and unfolded it. It was a missing corner of the map. On it was a picture of the pyramid and some notes describing a golden treasure.

"That's how he knew." She sighed. "This piece does show another tunnel out of here. But Freddy will be long gone by the time we get out."

Rosie and Rolland emerged from the tunnel to a high rock shelf at the back of the pyramid. Feeling exhausted, they sat down on the edge.

"How did he follow us, Rolland?" Rosie slouched. "I'm so tired."

Suddenly, Rolland's ears perked up.

"Boy? What is it?"

In the distance, Rosie could see a small dot in the sky.

It was a hot air balloon! Someone waved to them from the basket. "Grandpa?" Rosie exclaimed.

"Good to see you two!" he hollered back. "Need a lift?"

"Yes, please!" she said.

He slowed the balloon so that it hovered directly above the ledge and then dropped a rope ladder. They climbed up, and Rosie gave him a big hug.

"How'd you know where to find us?" she asked.

"I noticed that my hat had been...borrowed," he said with a smile. "Find any treasure today?"

Rosie pouted. "It slipped through our fingers."

"Oh, I'm sorry to hear that," he said, squeezing her tight. "It looks like you two had quite the adventure, though. You will have to tell me everything." He moved to the side and pulled the ladder back up. "Let's go home."

The next day at show-and-tell, Ms. Fairfax called Freddy and Rosie to the front of the class.

"Freddy, go ahead."

"Well," Freddy began, "last night, I found this amazing treasure in a jungle pyramid! There were all these traps and ferocious animals...but I emerged victorious!"

"And can we see this incredible treasure?" Ms. Fairfax asked.

"Well, um, you see," Freddy began, "it's so valuable that my dad said I, uh, shouldn't bring it to school."

"Ah, that's quite the story. But next time, perhaps you could bring something that you can show us?" She turned to Rosie. "It's your turn, dear."

Rosie looked at Freddy. She sighed and placed her grandfather's hat on her head.

Show and Tell!

"This is my grandpa's hat."
She pulled out a picture.
"This is him. My grandpa says he loves telling people about his adventures. He's been all over the world, actually. He doesn't bring back very much, other than a few pictures, but he always wears this hat."
She smiled.
"It's his adventure hat."

As Rosie was leaving school, she felt a tap on her shoulder.

"It's just a dumb rock now," said Freddy, spitting the words. "Ever since I got it home, it's been broken or something. What did you do to it?"

Freddy let the rock roll out of his hand and then stomped off. "You carry it!"

Rosie watched him walk away. She stared over at the rock.

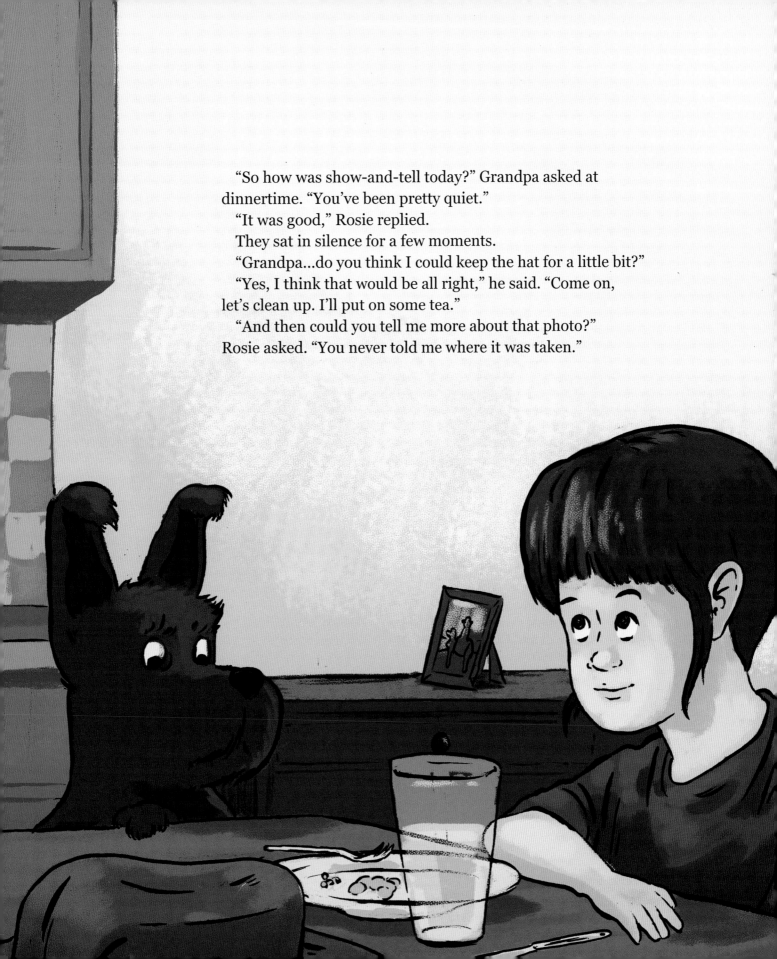

"So how was show-and-tell today?" Grandpa asked at dinnertime. "You've been pretty quiet."

"It was good," Rosie replied.

They sat in silence for a few moments.

"Grandpa...do you think I could keep the hat for a little bit?"

"Yes, I think that would be all right," he said. "Come on, let's clean up. I'll put on some tea."

"And then could you tell me more about that photo?" Rosie asked. "You never told me where it was taken."

Later that night, Rosie got ready to sleep. She closed her door and climbed into bed, with Rolland already comfortably settled at the end. She pulled the covers up and turned off the light. Moments passed. The room was dark and quiet.

A glow began to peek through the top of her schoolbag.

"Rolland...*look!*" she whispered.

The light grew brighter as it fought to get out of her closed bag. She went over—Rolland right behind her—unzipped the top, and pulled out the glowing golden rock.

The two friends sat together and looked forward to the adventures to come.

For Jenn,
and to everyone who encouraged me
along the way—thank you.

Text and illustrations © 2015 Jon Berg

All rights reserved. No part of this publication may be reproduced, stored in a retrieval system, or transmitted in any form or by any means, without the prior written permission of Owlkids Books Inc., or in the case of photocopying or other reprographic copying, a license from the Canadian Copyright Licensing Agency (Access Copyright). For an Access Copyright license, visit www.accesscopyright.ca or call toll-free to 1-800-893-5777.

Owlkids Books acknowledges the financial support of the Canada Council for the Arts, the Ontario Arts Council, the Government of Canada through the Canada Book Fund (CBF) and the Government of Ontario through the Ontario Media Development Corporation's Book Initiative for our publishing activities.

Published in Canada by
Owlkids Books Inc.
10 Lower Spadina Avenue
Toronto, ON M5V 2Z2

Published in the United States by
Owlkids Books Inc.
1700 Fourth Street
Berkeley, CA 94710

Library and Archives Canada Cataloguing in Publication

Berg, Jon, 1990-, author, illustrator
     Rosie & Rolland in the legendary show-and-tell / written and illustrated by Jon Berg.

ISBN 978-1-77147-058-2 (bound)

     I. Title. II. Title: Rosie and Rolland in the legendary show-and-tell.

PS8603.E673R68 2015   jC813'.6   C2014-905499-8

Library of Congress Control Number: 2014947494

Edited by: John Crossingham
Designed by: Barb Kelly

Manufactured in Dongguan, China, in November 2014, by Toppan Leefung Packaging & Printing (Dongguan) Co., Ltd.
Job #BAYDC13

A   B   C   D   E   F

Publisher of Chirp, chickaDEE and OWL
www.owlkidsbooks.com